To the memory of Dr Francoise Henri,
who made pictures come alive – *M.A.*

For Katie and Lucy – *G.M.*

MARIO'S ANGELS

A story about the artist Giotto

Mario's Angels copyright © Frances Lincoln Limited 2006
Text copyright © Mary Arrigan 2006
Illustrations copyright © Gillian McClure 2006

First published in Great Britain in 2006 by
Frances Lincoln Children's Books, 4 Torriano Mews
Torriano Avenue, London NW5 2RZ
www.franceslincoln.com

Distributed in the USA by Publishers Group West

Photographic acknowledgements:
Nativity by Giotto di Bondone and photograph of
Scrovegni Chapel, Padua © photo Scala, Florence, 1990

British Library Cataloguing in Publication Data
available on request

ISBN 10: 1-84507-404-1
ISBN 13: 9-781-84507-404-3

Set in Spectrum
Printed in Singapore

1 3 5 7 9 8 6 4 2

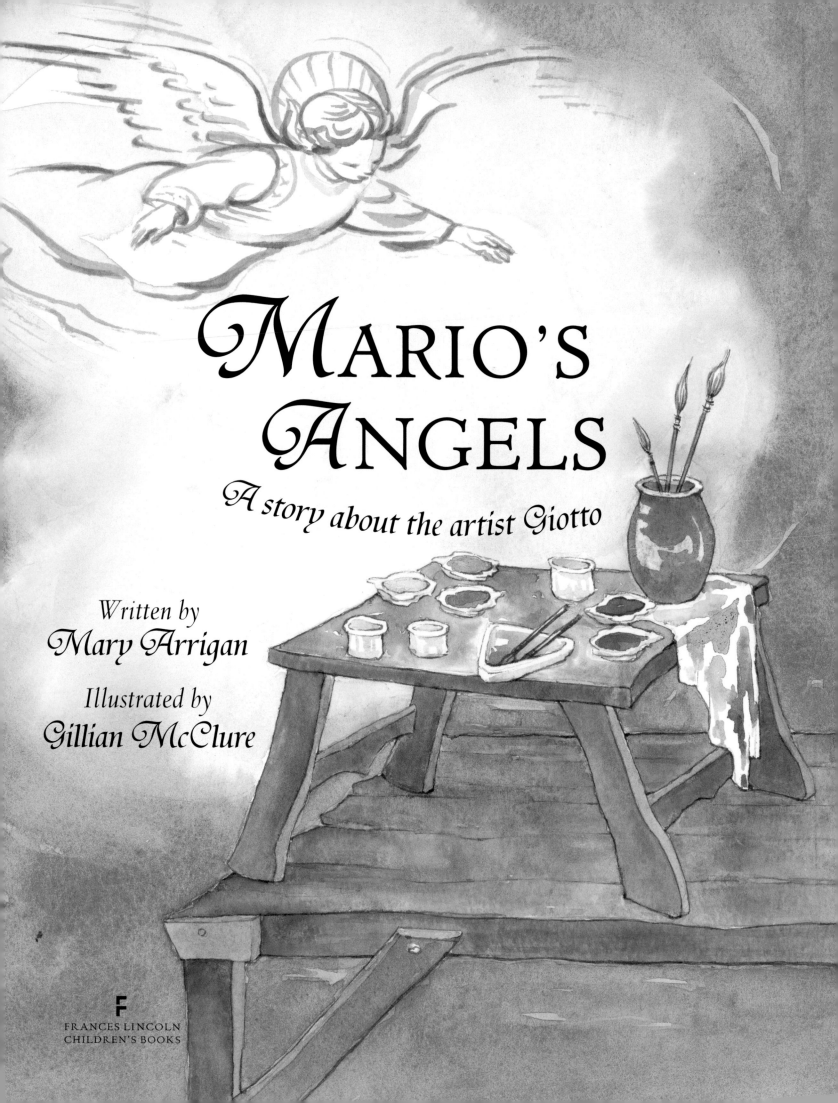

MARIO'S ANGELS

A story about the artist Giotto

Written by
Mary Arrigan

Illustrated by
Gillian McClure

F
FRANCES LINCOLN
CHILDREN'S BOOKS

"Good morning, Mario," said Giotto.

"Hello, Mister Giotto," said Mario.
"What are you doing?"

"I'm painting a fresco," replied Giotto.

"What is a fresco?" asked Mario.

"It's a picture painted on to a wall,"
said Giotto. "First I put on plaster
and then I paint on top of the plaster
while it is still wet."

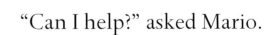

"Can I help?" asked Mario.

"Er, no thanks, Mario,"
said Giotto.

"Those people look real, Mister Giotto," said Mario. "I've never seen real people in paintings before."

"I like my people to look real and move about," said Giotto.

"I'm real," said Mario, "and I move about a lot. Can I be in your fresco?"

Giotto shook his head.
"Sorry, Mario," he said,
"but perhaps when you are older
you can be a fresco painter."

The big door creaked open.

"Look, Mister Giotto," said Mario.
"It's Father Prior. I suppose he has
come to look at your fresco."

"I suppose he has," said Giotto.
He wiped his hands on a rag and
climbed down from his platform.

"Is Father Prior in your fresco,
Mister Giotto?" asked Mario. "He's old
and fat, but he moves about. Is he
one of your people?"

"Ssshhh," whispered Giotto. "No, Mario.
Father Prior is not in my fresco."

"What do you think, Father Prior?" asked Giotto. "Do you like my fresco?"

"It has real people in it," said Mario, "people who move about and look happy and sad."

"Hmmm," said Father Prior. "Hmmm. There's something missing."

"Something missing?" exclaimed Giotto. "What could be missing?"

"Something in the sky," said Father Prior. "The sky is too dull. Fix the sky."

Giotto went out into the garden.

"What's wrong, Mister Giotto?" asked Mario. "You look sad."

"I am sad, Mario," replied Giotto. "I don't think Father Prior likes my fresco."

"It's a brilliant fresco, Mister Giotto," said Mario.

"The sky is wrong," muttered Giotto.

"I'll help you fix the sky, Mister Giotto," said Mario.
"There are lots of things you could put in it.
You could have a sunset."

"Too bright," said Giotto.

"Clouds, then," said Mario.

"Too fluffy," said Giotto.

"Rain," said Mario. "Nice big raindrops."

"Too dreary," sighed Giotto.

"I"ll think about it tonight, Mister Giotto," said Mario,
"and tomorrow I'll help you fix your sky."

That night, Mario played with his baby sister, Bianca, as she crawled around the kitchen floor. When his father came home from work in the bakery, he swept Bianca up into the air.

"My little angel," he laughed.

"She looks as if she has no feet," laughed Mario.

"Angels don't need feet." said his father. "Angels fly."

Mario thought for a moment.

"That's it!" he cried. "I know exactly what Mister Giotto can do!"

Later on, he smiled in his sleep as he dreamed of a wonderful sky.

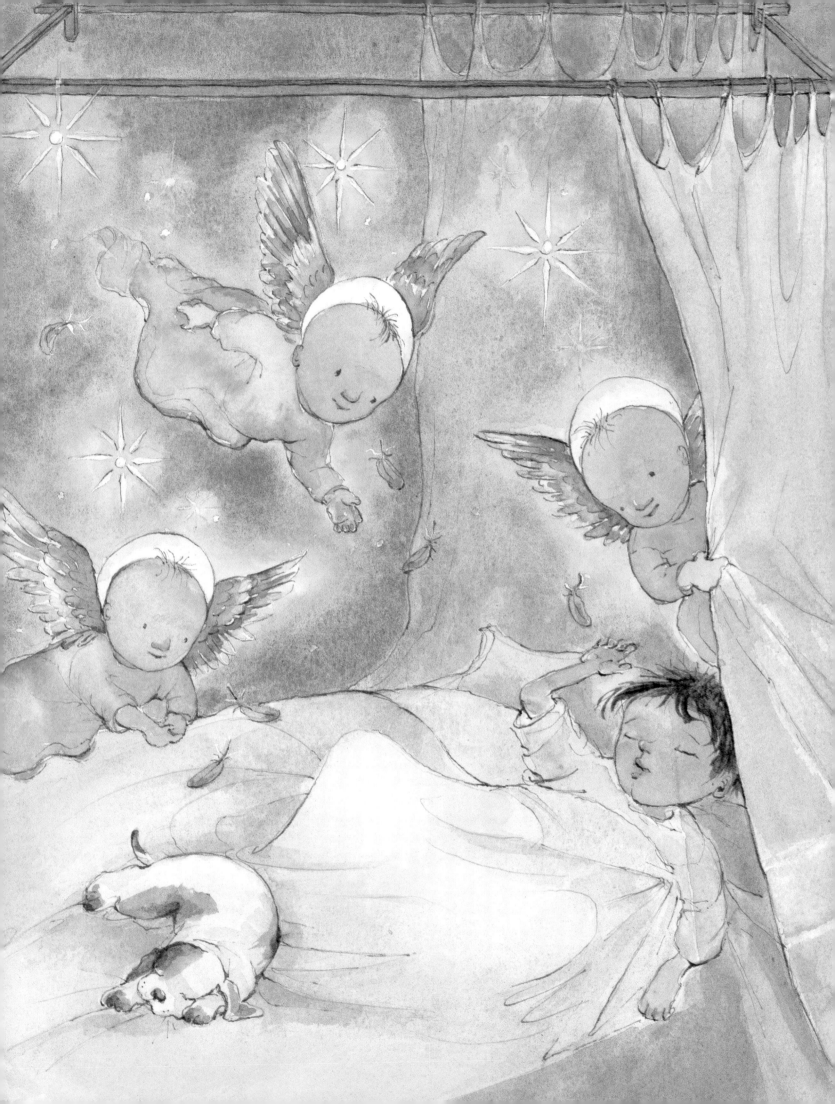

Next morning, Mario didn't even wait for breakfast.
He charged through the town with his great idea
for Mister Giotto's sky.

"What's your hurry, young Mario?"
shouted the neighbours.
But Mario didn't stop to explain.

"Angels, Mister Giotto!" exclaimed Mario.

"Angels, Mario?" said Giotto.

"Angels with real faces," said Mario.
"Angels who move about."

Giotto smiled.

"Mario," he beamed, "you are a genius.
Let's go and sketch some angels straight away."

"Where will we find them?" asked Mario.

"You can be my angels, Mario," laughed Giotto.
"I'll draw you."

Out in the garden,
Mario jumped and danced while
Giotto sketched him.

"But don't draw my feet," said Mario.
"Angels don't need feet because they fly."
And he told Giotto about his baby sister Bianca.

"Can I be in your fresco now, Mister Giotto?" asked Mario,
when Giotto had finished drawing him.

Giotto laughed.

"Of course, Mario," he said. "I'll put your angels
into all my frescoes!"

On Christmas morning, Mario peeped out of the door.

"Here he comes, Mister Giotto," he cried. "Father Prior is coming!"

Giotto took a deep breath. "Let's hope he will like my fresco now," he said.

Father Prior looked up at the fresco and gasped.

"Oh my!" he said. "This ... is wonderful. I have never seen a finer Nativity. This is absolutely splendid. It makes Christmas come alive."

"And it has angels," said Mario proudly. "*My* angels."

About Giotto

Giotto di Bondone was born near Florence in about 1266. At that time artists in Italy painted in a very stiff style. The figures of people they painted showed no emotion and were very still. Giotto changed all this. His people looked sad or happy, and as if they were moving about, just like real people. Giotto's fame spread far and wide and other artists were inspired by his realistic paintings. People now think of him as the father of European painting.

Giotto's best-known works are wall-paintings, also called *frescoes*. The most famous of these can be seen in the Scrovegni Chapel, a small church in Padua in Northern Italy, where his *Nativity* scene is much admired.

Nativity, Giotto di Bondone

Scrovegni Chapel, Padua

About frescoes

In Giotto's time, artists who were commissioned to decorate the inside walls
of big churches and palaces used the *fresco* technique.

The word 'fresco' is Italian for 'fresh', because the artist applied wet plaster
to the walls. He spread several layers of fine plaster over the wall surface and
drew his 'cartoon' or drawing on the top layer. Then he applied a final layer
of very smooth plaster on top. Last of all, he applied his paint to the wet
top layer. He only put as much plaster on the wall as he could paint in one day.
This method bonded the fresco to the wall.

So painting a fresco was a very slow job for Giotto. He needed a lot of patience.